Tongue of a Bird

by Ellen McLaughlin

A Samuel French Acting Edition

SAMUEL FRENCH

FOUNDED 1830

New York Hollywood London Toronto

SAMUELFRENCH.COM

ISBN   978-0-573-62707-1   Printed in U.S.A.   #22746

IMPORTANT BILLING AND CREDIT REQUIREMENTS
All producers of TONGUE OF A BIRD *must* give credit to the Author of the Play in all programs distributed in connection with performances of the Play and in all instances in which the title of the Play appears for purposes of advertising, publicizing or otherwise exploiting the Play and/or a production. The name of the Author *must* also appear on a separate line, on which no other name appears, immediately following the title, and *must* appear in size of type not less than fifty percent the size of the title type.
In addition, the following *must* appear in all advertising and programs used in connection with performances of the Play:

TONGUE OF A BIRD was originally presented as a staged reading by New York Stage and Film Company and the Powerhouse Theatre at Vassar in Association with Ron Kastner, July 1996
Originally Commissioned by Center Theatre Group of Los Angeles Gordon Davidson, Artistic Director

TONGUE OF A BIRD was originally produced by Intiman Theatre in 1997
Seattle, Washington
Warner Shook, Artistic Director; Laura Penn, Managing Director

TONGUE OF A BIRD was produced in New York by the Public Theatre/New York Shakespeare Festival in March 1999
George C. Wolfe, Producer

THE JOSEPH PAPP PUBLIC THEATER/ NEW YORK SHAKESPEARE FESTIVAL

Producer
GEORGE C. WOLFE

Artistic Producer
ROSEMARIE TICHLER

Managing Director
MARK LITVIN

AND

THE MARK TAPER FORUM

Artistic Director/Producer
GORDON DAVIDSON

PRESENT

TONGUE OF A BIRD

By **ELLEN McLAUGHLIN**

With
**CHERRY JONES   SHARON LAWRENCE   MELISSA LEO
JULIA McILVAINE   ELIZABETH WILSON**

Scenic Design	**RACHEL HAUCK**
Costume Design	**CANDICE CAIN**
Lighting Design	**MARY LOUISE GEIGER**
Original Music/Sound Design	**GINA LEISHMAN**
Sound System Design	**APPLIED AUDIO TECHNOLOGIES**
Production Dramaturg	**JOHN DIAS**
Production Stage Manager	**NANCY ELIZABETH VEST**

Directed by **LISA PETERSON**

Senior Director, External Affairs
MARGARET M. LIOI

Associate Producer
WILEY HAUSAM

Artistic Associate
BRIAN KULICK

Associate Producer
BONNIE METZGAR

General
Press Representative
CAROL R. FINEMAN

General
Manager
MICHAEL HURST

Casting
**JORDAN THALER/CINDY TOLAN
STANLEY SOBLE**

This production is made possible, in part, by a generous grant from AT&T.

Tongue of a Bird *was originally presented as a staged reading by New York Stage and Film Company and the Powerhouse Theatre at Vassar in Association with Ron Kastner, July 1996. It was originally commissioned by Center Theatre Group of Los Angeles: Gordon Davidson, Artistic Director.* Tongue of a Bird *was originally produced in 1997 by Intiman Theatre, Seattle, Washington: Warner Shook, Artistic Director; Lara Penn, Managing Director.*

CHARACTERS

MAXINE: Mid- to late thirties. A search and rescue pilot. Solitary, ironic and guarded.

DESSA: Mid- to late thirties. Charlotte's mother. Tough, without self-pity and utterly focused.

ZOFIA: Early to mid-seventies. Maxine's grandmother, Evie's mother. A Polish exile, survivor of the 1939 Nazi invasion. Visionary, difficult and wise.

CHARLOTTE: Twelve. Dessa's daughter. Canny, bold and slightly malicious.

EVIE: Roughly Maxine's age. Maxine's dead mother. Cool, wry and lucid.

TIME
Mid-winter.

PLACE
The Adirondacks.

<u>Note on the text:</u>

One speech follows another, unless a speech includes a slash (/), which indicates that the next speaker interrupts the previous speaker at this point. As in:

MAXINE. —I don't think that had anything / to do with—
DESSA. —They were laughing.

In this case, Dessa's cue word is "anything" and she talks over the end of Maxine's speech.

This play is dedicated to
Jane Lincoln Taylor
and to the memory of Sigrid Wurschmidt,
dear friends who gave me sight and
courage.

ACT I

Scene 1. Globe.

(In the darkness we hear an unidentifiable sound. Lights reveal a child's large globe, spinning. A small figure appears, dressed in brilliant white, perhaps completely wrapped in gauze. The figure approaches the globe and leans over it, peering at it. The figure then places a finger on the globe, stopping it.

As the figure leans in to look at the place it has pointed to, the globe's colors fade, as if frosting over into white. The figure looks down, looks out and then moves on, batting the globe into motion as it goes. The globe spins again, regaining its colors.)

Scene 2. The Buzzing.

(MAXINE stands in a high place. She looks down.)

MAXINE. There's a girl, this is me, standing at a high window, looking down. She tells herself: you will remember this. And I do. I remember everything. But I don't remember why

I remember this. It is morning and I'm looking down across a vast landscape and I've lost something which I think I will spot from this height. The farther up you are the more you see. This is true, I have learned this since ... and it's like a flicker of light sometimes, perhaps the glint of a climber's goggles, the quirk, almost indiscernible, of the wrong color, the dropped glove, the upturned shoe. These things, the slight, the rare, I see them as others don't, I am gifted—and here, there's something about this memory, but I can't ...

A fly, I know, is buzzing up the window, a trapped fly, going up the air, which it finds strangely hard and unyielding, going up when it means to be going out. This is crucial but I don't know why. Perhaps it just tells me the season, which must be late autumn, a time when flies are dying in just this way, going up when they mean to be going out. And it seems to me that all nature is dying on this day. Except me, who stands and watches.

So there's the fly and there's the landscape, dropped like a platter below me.

I see it as if I were above it, looking down over the back of my own blond head. I see most of my past this way, remembered with a detachment which looks coolly down on a child I am, experiencing some dreadful thing, which I experienced but didn't, and experience again in recalling it, but don't.

There is that girl, who is me, so far below me, who might have lived my life if I hadn't left her there and come up here to watch her. *(Smiles.)* I was so terribly good at that. A trick I learned so early.

So I became a flyer.

But she asked me to remember this. So I look down with her on the bald hills of some uncertain autumn, and we hear the fly and we wait.

Scene 3. Dessa.

(Sound of a fly buzzing becomes the sound of planes droning. An airplane hangar, denoted by the light cast from high windows and a rickety table where MAXINE and DESSA sit with their coats on, holding paper cups of coffee.)

DESSA. —They told me you were the one who doesn't give up. So I'm asking you.

MAXINE. They haven't given up, they're—

DESSA. —Yes they have. They look at me sideways when I come in—everybody runs, pretends to be doing something—

MAXINE. —I really think—

DESSA. —Look at them, unscrewing engines and shit—that guy, Robbie Something—

MAXINE. —Robbie DaCaprio—

DESSA. —He says he's going to be up all day looking for my daughter. I came in, he's sitting there eating soup—

MAXINE. —They have to eat—

DESSA. —Playing with his game-boy computer thingie—

MAXINE. —They have to come down occasionally, if only to get / gas—

DESSA. —And they're sitting around the table, all of them, laughing—

MAXINE. —I don't think that had anything / to do with—

DESSA. —They were laughing.

(Pause.)

MAXINE. I really don't think they've given up. It's just that it's been more than a week—

DESSA. —Eleven days, four hours *(she looks at her watch),* twenty-five minutes, no, twenty-six, and twelve, thirteen seconds, no, fourteen ... fifteen ...

MAXINE. You realize you'd be hiring me. It's not free.

(DESSA takes out an antique watch.)

DESSA. That's what I got. Heirloom. I got no more money. I spent it on posters and stuff, this asshole detective, Carl What's-his-face, the milk cartons—
MAXINE. —Do the milk cartons / cost ... ?—
DESSA. —But I figure it's a plane that's going to—'cause if you could just see her—And the money's just—'cause I don't have time to waste, she's —I've been emptying out my ... So you can have the, this, there's still some money, I've just got to get it out of the bank, just ... I got your name and called you and I came here right away so I just picked up the watch ... *it doesn't matter* ... I'm sitting in that fucking house all day, all night, I'm looking at all this shit, these *things*, and you can have anything, come over, take a look, in fact, do me a favor, rent a U-Haul, like a huge one, pull it up outside the door and just start loading it up, couch, T.V., oven mitts, shampoo bottles, bath mats, clocks, celery sticks, just take it—and then get some suction thing, some supersonic vacuum thing, park the hose at the front door and get the, the, everything, the air, the dust on the walls, between the cracks, the sounds left over in there, and, while you're at it, *me*—yeah, suck me right up out of that place and then the house itself after me, like in some cartoon, if you can do that, porch, bannister, walls and windows, get it all, don't leave anything, just a hole, just nothing, not even a hole, nothing, and drive away. If you can find her, if that would help find her, 'cause I'm telling you, whatever it takes, I don't give a shit anymore.
I just want her back. I just want my daughter back.

(Pause. MAXINE slides the watch back to her across the table.)

MAXINE. I'll need some money later for gas.

Scene 4. Babcia.

(ZOFIA's house, denoted by an ancient armchair, a side table and a small light, covered with dust. ZOFIA is sitting, staring intently straight ahead. MAXINE enters, carrying a laundry bag.)

MAXINE. Babcia?

(MAXINE drops the bag.)

ZOFIA. *(Slightly startled.)* I thought you were the bird.
MAXINE. What bird?
ZOFIA. There is a bird down the chimney, oh, such a terrible omen, see the black wing marks? The soot all over everywhere? Beat, beat, beat against the walls all night, so frightened. I think she maybe broke herself trying to get out.
MAXINE. Do you want me to find her?
ZOFIA. No, no, I got her out. *(Confused.)* I thought I did. *(She remembers.)* I did. Yes. I put the blanket *(she makes the gesture),* so like that, she was flapping and beating in there, her black wings, yes, I did, because I remember, yes. I stood at the door and ...

(ZOFIA makes the gesture of opening her arms and watching a bird take flight.)

MAXINE. So she's gone.
ZOFIA. Yes. And here you are. *(She really looks at MAXINE for the first time.)* Why?
MAXINE. I told you I was coming. This morning, you remember?
ZOFIA. I don't believe in telephones.

MAXINE. Nevertheless.

ZOFIA. Why have you come back to me?

MAXINE. What do you mean, I told you—*(ZOFIA nods toward the laundry bag.)* What? You think I could get all of my earthly possessions into a laundry bag?

ZOFIA. Yes.

(Silence.)

MAXINE. I'm sort of between places.

ZOFIA. What happened?

MAXINE. Oh ... *(She makes a gesture.)* I don't know. It didn't work out.

ZOFIA. I don't have room for you here.

MAXINE. What do you mean? That's all you've got—room.

ZOFIA. It's all filled up.

MAXINE. *(Laughs.)* With what? You've never even had furniture / here.

ZOFIA. *(Furious, slapping the arms of the chair.)* I have—!

MAXINE. —Well, yes. There is the *chair,* but nothing, almost nothing—

ZOFIA. —Space!

MAXINE. What?

ZOFIA. It's all filled up!

MAXINE. What?

ZOFIA. With space!

(Silence.)

MAXINE. Look, I won't be staying long. Just a few days. Just for the search.

ZOFIA. What is this?

MAXINE. I got another search. I'm going to be flying these mountains for awhile, until we find her of course.

ZOFIA. Who?

MAXINE. A girl.

ZOFIA. How young?

MAXINE. Twelve.

ZOFIA. How long has she been lost?

MAXINE. Eleven days.

ZOFIA. Eleven days? In this weather? Ach. She's frozen already.

MAXINE. Well, actually, I'm looking for a black pickup truck.

ZOFIA. *(Confused.)* She's driving ... ?

MAXINE. She was kidnapped. A man. She was hiking with some friends. Girl Scouts. She's standing on the edge of a clearing, and a truck drives out of nowhere, her friends watch her have a conversation, they can't see the man inside the truck, pickup truck, we don't know what make. Suddenly he reaches out and grabs her, drags her into the truck, drives away up into the mountains. All the roads out of there have been closed off since then, he can't have gotten out so he must have gone up. The police, the Mountain Rescue, the Civil Air Patrol, it's been a big thing. Her picture is all over the place. But it's been awhile and the weather's too tricky for the helicopters anymore and they're too expensive. So that's where I come in. Her mother heard about me.

ZOFIA. Twelve years old?

MAXINE. Yes.

(Pause.)

ZOFIA. *Biedny malutki ptaszek.*

MAXINE. What? *(ZOFIA shakes her head. MAXINE continues, writing in the dust of the table.)* Are there any clean sheets?

ZOFIA. There are always sheets. You know where. What are you doing?

MAXINE. Writing my name in the dust.

(ZOFIA slaps at MAXINE's hand.)

ZOFIA. I don't want your name all over my nice table.

MAXINE. It looks like nobody's cleaned since I was here last summer. Why don't you ever let What's-her-name come in and clean this place? She's offered dozens of times.

ZOFIA. That woman. She changes things.

MAXINE. Well, yes, she cleans them.

ZOFIA. Stop *looking* at everything. Who are you to look so much?

MAXINE. *(Gestures to the room.)* I have eyes. It's a problem.

ZOFIA. Ach.

MAXINE. I brought you cake.

ZOFIA. What kind?

MAXINE. *Czekolada.*

(MAXINE takes a slice of cake wrapped in a napkin out of her coat pocket. She unwraps it and hands it to ZOFIA.)

ZOFIA. Ah. *Ciastko czekoladowe.*
What is that smell in it? That dark smell? How nice.

MAXINE. I remembered, you see? Such a doting granddaughter.

ZOFIA. It was the strangest thing. All the children who arrived in New York off the first boat from Poland. Some rich woman sent cake to us, chocolate cake. And we stood on the dock and ate it. It was the first thing I tasted in America. Some ... what-do-you-call—eccentric millionaire woman, I forget her name, she sends all the children of the war cake. After that our troubles began. But at that time I thought, so this is what it will always be like here—chocolate cake and the salt air, and the sugar frosting on my wool gloves.

MAXINE. So that's why.

ZOFIA. Someone had thought of us. *(Pause.)* Only until you find her. So long you can stay. No more.

MAXINE. I wasn't planning on staying any longer.

ZOFIA. It's good.

MAXINE. What?

ZOFIA. That you can put your life into a ... everything you have you can hold in a ...

(ZOFIA can't find the word; she snaps her fingers with impatience.)

MAXINE. Laundry bag?

ZOFIA. No, not "laundry," not "bag" ... ach, *torebka...*

MAXINE. "Sack"?

ZOFIA. *(Relieved.) Sak! Sak, sak, sak!* Yes. That you can do that, you learned from me that. Yes. Good.

MAXINE. Oh, I'm not so sure anymore.

ZOFIA. Oh, yes. All you need you have to carry here. *(She taps her head.)* Because everything else they can take from you.

MAXINE. Who?

ZOFIA. Who takes? *(She laughs.)* The world. *(She gestures out.)* That. *(She taps her head.)* This is all you can take. When I was a little girl, walking out of Poland after the bombs ... the ones of us who were left. Ach. We took all the wrong things ... little spoons, a duck, a purple table runner ... We were so stupid. We would be holding all the wrong things for the rest of our lives, no matter where we went ... Ach. I would hold the little comb to my chest all night long on the boat across the ocean, because I cannot hold my mother's hand, never again. And I think, this will save me. This will be enough. A comb she gave me. Because her hand had been on it. This will save me. This thing.

MAXINE. Where is the comb?

ZOFIA. *(Smiles.)* I threw it in the ocean. It was not enough. The cup my dead father made for me, her glove ... seven silver buttons ... *(She makes a gesture of throwing.)* I walked off that boat with nothing in my hands. Like an animal. I made myself do that. Skin and bones and this. *(She touches her head. She gestures to the sack.)* What's in there?

MAXINE. Nothing much. Clothes. Some books.

ZOFIA. Throw it in the ocean!

MAXINE. Right.

ZOFIA. Throw them away! *(She laughs.)* Who needs them? Not even little girls. *(She looks out into the night.)* She was twelve?

MAXINE. Who?

ZOFIA. That little girl?

MAXINE. *(Not quite sure which girl they are talking about.)* Yes.

ZOFIA. She's probably dead by now.

Scene 5. Mama.

(A very dimly lit bedroom. MAXINE's old room in ZOFIA's house. Something is wrong. MAXINE is asleep in bed. She wakes, startled. A pause. She turns on the bedside light. A woman is hanging like a side of meat, her feet perhaps five feet from the ground. She is dressed in a stereotypical flight suit—leather dust coat, goggles and helmet. MAXINE gasps and turns off the light. Pause.)

MAXINE. Mama?

(Pause. MAXINE turns on the light. The figure is gone.)

Scene 6. Powder Blue.

(Airplane hangar. Predawn. DESSA is sifting through some photographs and papers she's brought for MAXINE. MAXINE enters, already exhausted, surprised to see DESSA.)

DESSA. I got another picture for you. It's the sixth grade class picture so it's not ... I mean, her hair is longer and she doesn't have the braces but still. And it's not really like her, the eyes, I think she's about to blink, she hates it, this picture, see she's standing next to this guy, Neil Kransky, she says he smells or something, see how she's leaning away a little bit. *(Laughs.)* I never noticed that, she's got these *opinions*, she *hates* this photo. See how tall she is, though? She's the tallest one in the back row. I keep thinking that's ... I keep thinking that's going to make a difference, you know? It's not ... it's not *rational* but ... *(Suddenly.)* Oh, Jeez, I almost forgot—the jacket she's wearing—it's *really* light blue—powder blue they call it—I went back to the store to look at it, they still had one—so it's not just light blue, like I told you, it's powder blue like—*(She looks around.)* Shit, I was going to bring in something that color—I could go buy the jacket, it's the same one, how about that?
MAXINE. No, that's O.K., I think I—
DESSA. —*(Pointing.)* Like *that.*
MAXINE. What?
DESSA. The sky right now.
MAXINE. *(Too quickly.)* O.K.
DESSA. No. *Look.* Not near where the sun's coming up. Further up.
MAXINE. *(Looking.)* O.K.
DESSA. Not where you're looking. Where I'm pointing.
MAXINE. *(Trying to oblige.)* Yeah. Right there. Got it.

DESSA. Shit, it's already changing. *(She takes MAXINE by the arm and pulls her over, then puts their heads next to each other.)* Where my finger is. Is it the same place for your eyes?

MAXINE. Close enough.

DESSA. Fuck, it's already changing. *That* color. Right there.

MAXINE. I see it. Very light blue.

(DESSA lets go of her abruptly.)

DESSA. It's changed. Not that color. What it *was*. Do you remember?

MAXINE. Yes.

DESSA. What it *was*.

MAXINE. Yes.

DESSA. Not what it is now.

MAXINE. Yes.

DESSA. Remember that.

MAXINE. Yes.

DESSA. That's the color of the jacket she has on.

It's brand new. *(Pause.)*

Go. It's light enough.

Scene 7. Charlotte.

(Day. MAXINE is in the cockpit of her plane, searching.)

MAXINE. Charlotte. Charlotte Hobart. I am looking for you. Serious girl, almost pretty, shy, quiet. A good girl. On your report card, your teacher writes: "She seems to be in love with nature. Rather romantic and solitary." I know the type. Always looking out of windows.

Twelve years old. What goes on in that head of yours?

Sex? What do you know about it? What you read in books? Movies? There is a kid in your class who punches your arm a lot and that does mean something. There is one day when you are alone with him in a barn and you find yourselves discussing religion. You lie on your backs and he lazily tosses a baseball straight up toward the rafters and catches it in his glove. Leather smacks neatly into leather. At that moment you say, "I think God exists in everything—the barn swallows, the straw, the dirt under my fingernails, your sneaker." And it so happens that his investigations into things have led him to the same conclusion. "Everything is sacred," he says. And there is a long silence because what now can be said? You lie there, not looking at each other, not touching each other either.

But then, you don't have to. *(Bang. Something hits the side of the plane.)*

It was as perfect as it gets. *(Bang.)*

What was that? A bird?

Life for you was as simple as a long plank to walk.

And at the end of it, this man. Is that right? *(Pause.)*

Bullshit, Maxine. What do you know about it? *(Pause.)*

Charlotte Hobart. What is being done to you?

What is being done to you—right now? *(Pause. Subdued.)*

Oh Jesus. *(A final bang, the loudest, on the window. MAXINE is startled back to reality. As irritated as she is frightened.)*

What the fuck *is* that?

Scene 8. Ta Da.

(Lights flicker. Suddenly, the girl, CHARLOTTE, sits beside MAXINE in the cockpit; bloody and dead but unperturbed, she looks out the window. MAXINE is surprised and horrified.)

CHARLOTTE. You found me. Ta da.
MAXINE. Jesus.
CHARLOTTE. Congratulations. Aren't you something.
MAXINE. Oh God, what's going on?

CHARLOTTE. Well, what *would* you do?

MAXINE. What?

CHARLOTTE. See, you can't even imagine.

MAXINE. Of course I can. This is, this is what I do.

CHARLOTTE. No it isn't. You make the search, you sometimes see something. Then you send the helicopter or whatever, right? *You never land.* It's all pretty pristine. You never have to deal with *this* for instance.

(CHARLOTTE draws a bloody finger down MAXINE's face.)

MAXINE. I hate this.

CHARLOTTE. Some hero.

MAXINE. So all right, since you're here. Maybe you can tell me.

CHARLOTTE. What?

MAXINE. Where are you? What is happening to you?

CHARLOTTE. Sometimes the quiet girls go completely mute. Isn't it provoking? Neither seen *nor* heard. Poof. They just vanish. No one can see them, even when they stand right in front of you. Like your mother.

MAXINE. What about her?

CHARLOTTE. You're so far-sighted now maybe you can only read suicide notes when they're printed out in huge stones and felled trees. Look. It says maybe "STOP LOOKING" or "GIVE UP comma I'M ALREADY DEAD."

MAXINE. That's not what's going on. Not this time.

CHARLOTTE. How do you know? Can you imagine what I'm going through?

MAXINE. Yes. I can imagine.

CHARLOTTE. *(Laughs.)* No you can't. Me and that Norman Rockwell boy in the barn? You wish, Honey.

MAXINE. I can imagine. Too well. Better than others. It keeps me up here. Looking longer. Past other people's threshold of hope. That thin line between hope and despair— mine's a longer suspension of disbelief. That's why I'm good.

CHARLOTTE. A tightrope walker after all.

MAXINE. Yes.

CHARLOTTE. Just like you dreamed of being when you were my age.

Don't you find yourself looking at your feet these days?

MAXINE. You never look at your feet. That's the trick.

CHARLOTTE. You've been looking lately. I've noticed.

MAXINE. Never.

CHARLOTTE. You have. You're stuck in the middle of the rope. Right smack in the middle. No going forward, no going back. Fright. Hits the best of them at your age. So you find yourself looking at your foot, and you know what? You're right. This is exactly, just exactly where your mother's foot slipped.

(CHARLOTTE disappears.)

MAXINE. No.

Scene 9. Demon Machine.

(MAXINE is in the airport hangar building. She is leaning against the coffee vending machine, obviously tired and cold.)

MAXINE. *(Beleaguered.)* Christ. *(She puts some change into the machine. A cup comes down, but lodges wrong, at an angle.)*

No, no, don't do this to me again. *(She starts to try to right the cup but isn't quick enough; the coffee starts pouring down and burns her hand.)*

Fucking *demon* machine.

(As the scalding liquid pours down, it runs all over the floor. MAXINE stands back to watch.)

MAXINE. Oh, tremendous. Lovely. All over the floor. And *coffee*, yet, not hot chocolate, as I requested. Ah, thank you so much. Are we finished? All done? *(Final spurt.)* All righty, then.
Shall we try again?

(She fishes in her pockets for change. As she does so, EVIE descends, looking as she usually does. She hangs behind MAXINE and about a foot above her head. MAXINE senses something and slowly turns. This is quite disturbing. She quickly looks around to see if anyone else is in the hangar. No one is. She looks back, then experiments. She puts her hands in front of her eyes for a moment, then looks again. Her mother is still there.)

MAXINE. All right, Maxine. Just fucking deal. Just fucking—*(Down to business.)* O.K. Get out of here. Shoo. Vamoose. Or at least—

(MAXINE walks over and reaches up for EVIE's foot. EVIE begins to ascend; MAXINE just barely has grasp of a foot. EVIE shakes her off and ascends just out of reach. MAXINE jumps. EVIE is out of range. She ascends slowly out of sight.)

MAXINE. *(Calling after EVIE.)* And you never flew a— YOU NEVER FLEW A PLANE IN YOUR ENTIRE LIFE, SO WHAT IS THIS GET-UP SUPPOSED TO ...
Ma? Mama? *(EVIE is gone. MAXINE looks around, shaken. She slowly walks to the coffee machine, begins to reach for change, and then suddenly punches it violently, hurting her hand. She holds her hand.)* Ow. *(To the machine.)* I'm sorry. Fuck. *(She leans her face against the machine.)*
I'm sorry.

(MAXINE begins to cry. She embraces the machine, crying.)

Scene 10. Flight.

(Night. MAXINE draws a chair up next to ZOFIA's.)

MAXINE. I think it's quite possible you haven't moved from that chair since I left you there, exactly like that, eighteen hours ago.

ZOFIA. It's possible. I guess it looks so to you. But it is not so simple ... My grandmother's mother, your, what?

MAXINE. Great-great-great-grandmother.

ZOFIA. Great, great, great ... She was one of the real, the first. The traveling women. They put henbane, an herb it is, rubbed it on the soles of their feet at night and *(she makes a gesture)* shoop, like a black bird. To the mountain. To dance.

MAXINE. You're saying she was a witch?

ZOFIA. *(Laughs.)* A witch. Yes. Traveling woman. *Czarownica.*

MAXINE. Huh.

ZOFIA. *(Laughs.)* You don't believe me. That's why I never told you. It doesn't matter. But I saw them, the traveling women. Like black swans across the sky one night. I was not supposed to see that. Her husband, he tried to tie her up on those nights, to a chair, to a bed, thick rope. And he would watch her. But always he would fall asleep and when he wakes up there is just this neat circle of the rope on the floor. What could he do? It was not so nice, maybe, what she was doing ... maybe ... But she couldn't help it. And then there was your mother. There was nothing I could do. *Masz to ve krwi.* It was the blood in her. Even when Evie was a little girl. Running always out into the night away from me. Me calling and calling for her as the dark came and she never comes until so late, even it was morning sometimes, and when she finally comes in she looks so like an animal, her eyes, ach, her eyes ... You look like that sometimes.

MAXINE. But I can fly.

ZOFIA. Oh, yes. The first one in a plane, but not the first one to fly, only the last one. It's maybe a disease. We pass it down.

MAXINE. It's the only thing that makes me happy. It's good.

ZOFIA. *(Nods.)* It's the blood. Mother to mother to mother. This *(she stamps her foot)* is not enough for any of us. We travel. Ach. *(She holds her head.)* We can't help it.

MAXINE. Babcia?

ZOFIA. Traveling too much.

MAXINE. You're traveling?

ZOFIA. *(Holds her head, as if to keep something in.)* Can't stay in. I try, it's very hard. So I think some day you will come here and look in the chair and, oh, nobody. No more.

MAXINE. Where will you be?

(ZOFIA shrugs, smiles.)

ZOFIA. Away. *(She closes her eyes. She takes MAXINE's hand.)* If you could see it. It's here. Just here.

(ZOFIA gestures to her closed eyes. She leans back. They hold hands for a moment, ZOFIA with her eyes still closed. MAXINE jerks her hand.)

MAXINE. Come back.
ZOFIA. No.
MAXINE. Come back.
ZOFIA. Why?
MAXINE. Because I can't go with you.
ZOFIA. Ach. Just let me...

(MAXINE takes ZOFIA by the shoulders and shakes her.)

MAXINE. No. No. No. Stop it.

ZOFIA. *(Opens her eyes, irritated.)* What's wrong with you?

MAXINE. I'm not going to just *watch* ... You can't expect me to just *watch* while you ... I don't want to lose you. Not yet.

ZOFIA. But you will lose me. It's how it happens. There comes a day. No one will find me. *(Pause.)* Some things cannot be found.

MAXINE. And some things can.

(Pause.)

ZOFIA. Why do you have to find her?

MAXINE. *(At a loss.)* Because it's important.

ZOFIA. What if she is only dead?

MAXINE. Even so. There's a difference I can make. Even if she's dead. It's the difference between catastrophe, the chaos of this horrible, senseless event, and something else. Not tragedy exactly, but ... It's important. That I do this. Search.
I can't explain it to you.

ZOFIA. What's lost is lost. You run out into *that*? *(She gestures.)* You get yourself lost in *that*? *(Another gesture.)* Ach. You cannot expect anyone to come looking for you. These things happen. It's a terrible world.

MAXINE. But you *can* expect that. You *can* expect someone to come looking for you. We owe that to each other. At least that much.
And I'm good at it.

ZOFIA. This world. Ach. This world, I think, wants to lose all her children and forget them. She is so good at losing. She is a mother who puts her children out of doors to die and forgets them as she turns to make more. We tap on the windows and call her name but the night is cold and she has turned away. So we run into the darkness and hug our sides and suck our dirty fingers for the memory of food. She will not take us back again no matter how we cry. Time goes by and we get older and we forget the warmth of her house, the taste of her bread, and soon we stop crying for them. Anything, I think,

can be borne. "Catastrophe," "tragedy" ... Whatever you want
to call it. It doesn't matter.
We are all put out of house and forgotten.
    MAXINE. This one girl. I will find her. I can do that.

Scene 11. Tongues.

*(MAXINE's room. Night. EVIE, the figure, is hanging above
    her, as before. MAXINE stares at her. Silence.)*

    MAXINE. All right. How does this work? Are you going
to talk to me? *(Pause.)* I guess I'll get used to you. Like some
absurd empty piñata that everyone forgot to take down. ·
(Trying another approach.) Since you're here, Ma, about your
mother ... what gives? I mean she seems to be ... like she's
doing some aerial, imaginary tour of the globe before she ... I
mean it's not really that simple, but she does seem to be going
somewhere ...
    EVIE. You know where.
    MAXINE. Oh, so it is that simple. *(Pause.)*
How many times did you try to kill yourself?
    EVIE. Seven. Eight. Seven. Nine? Does it matter?
    MAXINE. Oh, let's say nine. That sounds good. Like a
cat.
Am I making you up?
    EVIE. You're asking me?
    MAXINE. I guess I didn't realize how obsessed I was with
Earhart.
    EVIE. That's only the most obvious part of this.
    MAXINE. What do you have on under your coat?
    EVIE. Cut me open and find out. I'm your piñata.
    MAXINE. I can't. I think it's feathers.
    EVIE. Could be.
    MAXINE. Damp, matted feathers. Go away.

EVIE. You'll never find out anything if you're so afraid.
Chicken.

(EVIE begins to ascend, making clucking sounds.)

MAXINE. I'm not afraid of you. *(EVIE halts in her ascent.)* How could I be? You're just embarrassing more than anything else.

EVIE. You used to be. Afraid.

MAXINE. I'm sure I was. I was a little kid. All I knew was that you were mad.

EVIE. "Mad." How you flatter me. Sounds so romantic. Why not "crackers," why not "loony tunes"? Why not "My crazy fucking mother drove me nuts"?

MAXINE. It's what I was told. "Mad woman." "Sent away."

EVIE. "Away." Lovely. It sounds like a white place, like a plate, where all the mad women lie, waiting for judgment day. Mouths open and stopped up, tongues flat and silent ...

MAXINE. Right, Ma. Cooked meat. Pigs' tongues under apples.

EVIE. Cooked, yes, but not apples on our tongues. Black rubber. It tasted of nightmare factories. And you bite down hard. So that when the electricity courses through your soft brain the scream you scream goes meaningless and tiny into the piece of dull night you hold between your dangerous animal teeth. We bit and bit, grinning like the lit skeletons we became.

MAXINE. So you were one of them.

EVIE. Oh, yes. One of the many. Quite the little unhinged sorority. Lining the cots waiting for the daily execution. In our identical thin gowns. And afterwards, all our open mouths, like holes ripped in sheets and nothing coming out, nothing going in. We would walk up and peer into each other just to make sure. You know what a wild bird's tongue looks like? Not your nice birds, I'm talking about the ones you shoo off the garden, the greasy, sinister types—grackles, starlings—the types who steal from nice birds' nests and shriek and dive at

the house cats. Look at their tongues—black, flattened, moving splinters.
And the sounds they make with tongues like that. Horrible. In all of our open mouths. Imagine.

MAXINE. I wanted you to be different.

EVIE. Ah, no. There was never any difference between us. And when the treatments began, we knew for sure. We are all the same woman, that thrashing body on the table, biting rubber. You talk about "madness." No, my darling. Much, much simpler, much less grand. For instance, you're looking up at me now, and let me tell you something: You're right. I'm exactly what you look like.

MAXINE. Family resemblance.

EVIE. Oh. More than that. Just another flight-bound, black-tongued thing.

(EVIE ascends out of view.)

MAXINE. *(Calling after her.)* Forget it, Ma. I'm not scared of you anymore. You're just something I made up to spook myself.

EVIE. *(Out of sight.)* Just another greasy-feathered bird.

MAXINE. FUCK YOU! I'm *nothing* like you.

(Sound of wet wings.)

Scene 12. Earhart.

(MAXINE in the cockpit, searching.)

MAXINE. I dress my mother like you, Amelia. What is that about?
Amelia Earhart. Air Heart. Airheart. *(She laughs.)*
One thing I know, Amelia. I would have found you. Weeks they looked for you, all those air force yahoos, the largest air search in history. Not a trace. Hundreds of square miles of gray slate

water and no you. I would have found you. Because I know
you. I could see it in those eyes of yours. Photo after photo of
you, standing in front of planes as if you were guarding them,
that obliging beauty, that squint, that smile, that lovely
preoccupied air. You weren't there. The drug is what you see.
I know that drug. It's coursing through my veins right now.
It's solitude taken to the utmost extreme. You hear a snap and
yes, complete disconnection from the world. What wings do.
Abandon.

When I say I remember everything I'm lying. I don't remember
my mother. Memories only begin after her death, and then they
rear up in Technicolor and just won't quit. But before that, just
... nothing ... silence. Blind, aching void. And there is very little
evidence to assert that she *did* exist, that woman, except for me,
I suppose, who must have come from somewhere. She left no
trace, no trail, not a mark on this world apparently, no more
than a water bug leaves on the surface of a lake.

It would seem that my mother never wrote a letter in her life,
not a grocery list, I have never, in fact, seen her signature.

I have no memory of her voice, her touch, the true color of her
eyes, the way she laughed, if she ever laughed ... I look for
memories of her inside me and find nothing, no likeness, no
scent, except perhaps here, in the air. Airheart ...

Because you came here too, didn't you, Mama? Countless
times. Shot as if from a cannon out of yourself. Nothing and
no one, not even you, could hold you in. Disappeared ...

The search continues. For you, whoever you were ...

I have so little to go on. The only thing you bequeathed to this
earth was me, Mama. I am your bread crumb trail. *(She looks
at her hands.)* My bones, my sinews, every single part of me
... including this *(she raps her head with her knuckles),* which
is what? Just some bomb you set ticking before you stepped
off the face of the world? ... You left no traces on this earth
except me, Mama, your unwilling shadow, who can do nothing
now but limp down your tracks sniffing the air and wondering
what strange woods you have brought me to.

Scene 13. Winter.

(Airplane hangar. Night. MAXINE enters, exhausted, another day gone. DESSA is sitting at the table wearing her coat, waiting for her. They don't have to say anything; DESSA knows. Silence.)

DESSA. At least it hasn't rained or something. 'Cause you got to find her before it rains or something. Before the snow melts 'cause the black truck—it'll only show up against the snow. That's what I figure. The black against the white. That shows up well, right? You would see that. The truck.

MAXINE. Yeah. That's what I figure too.

DESSA. It's better if it's white. The snow. It's better. Even though it's cold. She's got that jacket and the snow boots from Christmas, they're good. She'll be warm. I know she took her gloves. All the girls said she was wearing them—the thermal what-do-you-call-it, some kind of warm plastic, they're waterproof and everything. She's always out all day in those. That's what these guys *(gestures around the room vaguely)*, they don't understand, I'm always calling to her to come in, she'll freeze to death ... but she won't until she's good and ready. She's like that. That's the thing I know about her. I'm always calling and calling out the back door. And when she's good and ready she comes in. She always comes in.

MAXINE. That's good to know.

DESSA. I hope spring never comes. I need the snow. Until you find her. I need the snow.

(Pause.)

MAXINE. Mrs. Hobart, / I really—

DESSA. —NO. *(Long pause.)* I'm not even going to take

her library books back. And they're overdue. Eight days now. She'll kill me when she gets back. She's never had an overdue book in her life. She's just like that.
But I can't ... do it. She's going to have to come back and return them herself ... I can never get across to her—she's so *serious* ... I keep telling her, keep them if you like them, keep them a few days more, just hang onto them ... It's such a *little* crime ... to keep something you love ... just a few days more.

(Pause.)

MAXINE. Have you eaten anything today? *(DESSA shakes her head.)*
You need to eat. Even if you can't feel hunger. I could stand a beer. How about we go out someplace? *(DESSA looks outside.)*
It's night. Nothing to see until morning.

(Pause.)

DESSA. *(Quiet, staring out.)* Fires.

(Pause.)

MAXINE. All right. But I need to eat something first. Then you can come up with me for awhile. *(DESSA tries to contain her surprise and exhilaration.)*
We'll look for fires.

(They leave.)

Scene 14. That Story.

(DESSA and MAXINE in the cockpit. They look out their re-spective windows. Night. DESSA is giddy, MAXINE amused.)

DESSA. Oh, God. Finally. To be *doing* something.

MAXINE. I don't know how much you can *see* ...

DESSA. I can't see a fucking thing. *(They laugh.)* I mean, how can you even fly? What are you, nuts? Not that I want you to *land* or anything, I mean, please don't, but really, where *is* anything?

MAXINE. You see that ridge there? The stand of trees along the top, it's like a knife edge?

DESSA. *(Laughing.)* Nope.

MAXINE. And then there's a little line, it used to be a log-ging road, it goes down, I always think it looks like a woman's profile.

DESSA. Yeah, well, whatever. Eagle eyes. I guess that's why you can do this for a living.

MAXINE. Why I get the big bucks.

DESSA. Yeah, right.

(They laugh.)

MAXINE. But really, I couldn't do this kind of night fly-ing anywhere else. I know these mountains pretty well. Better than anyplace. I love them.

DESSA. Yeah?

MAXINE. They're like, I don't know, I haven't lived here for years, but whenever I dream, this is the landscape. It goes deep, this place.

DESSA. You grow up out here?

MAXINE. Yeah. My grandmother raised me. I stay with her when I come back.

DESSA. *(Looking out the window.)* And you were happy here?

MAXINE. Actually, I think I was pretty miserable. *(They laugh.)* But I still like the mountains.

DESSA. Where was your mother?

MAXINE. She was kind of ... around sometimes, but ... she committed suicide when she was about my age.

DESSA. How old were you when she did that?

MAXINE. Six, I think. Maybe five. Small. Four? Somewhere in there.

DESSA. Uh huh.

MAXINE. A long time ago. I never knew her. She was mostly gone.

(Pause.)

DESSA. How did she kill herself?

MAXINE. What? Oh. She tried a lot of times, a lot of ways.

DESSA. Which one worked?

MAXINE. Um. I don't really know. And now my grandmother, the only one who really knows, she doesn't remember—

DESSA. —That doesn't seem likely—

MAXINE. —Or she just doesn't want to tell me.

DESSA. I think pills.

MAXINE. What?

DESSA. I've been thinking about pills. 'Cause I'm chicken and I don't want to make a mess. I don't know why I care, since I wouldn't have to clean it up. For once. But I'm pretty persnickety. Tidy.

MAXINE. You're thinking about killing yourself?

DESSA. Well lately, yeah.

(Pause.)

MAXINE. I'm probably not the person to talk to about this.

DESSA. Oh sure. Of course. *(Pause.)*

I mean, don't worry, or anything. I just *think* about it. I find it, you know, comforting ... That I could, you know, *do* ... something—to, uh, express my general, uh, disappointment with ...

MAXINE. God?

DESSA. Yeah, well ... Whoever's in charge. *(Pause.)* Thanks.

MAXINE. For what?

DESSA. For not saying *(cheerleader)* "Hey, buck up, Mrs. Hobart. Heck, we'll find her, you bet. Don't get so down in the dumps."

(Pause.)

MAXINE. I would like very much to find your daughter.

DESSA. Yeah.

Don't want to ruin that perfect record. *(Bad pause.)*

You know that's why I hired you.

MAXINE. What?

DESSA. I thought you were lucky. Shiny like a new coin.

MAXINE. Yeah. That's me. Lucky, lucky, lucky ... so lucky. *(Pause.)*

Don't kill yourself, please.

DESSA. Why not?

MAXINE. I'd be very bummed out. *(They laugh.)* Really. "Hey, buck up, Mrs. Hobart"—

DESSA. —You can call me Dessa—

MAXINE. —"Buck up, Dessa."

DESSA. Yeah? Say it.

MAXINE. Say what?

DESSA. "We're going to ..."

MAXINE. "We're going to ..."

DESSA. Go on.

MAXINE. "We're going to find your daughter."

DESSA. Oh man, you fucking well better.

Go champ. Defend your title. *(Pause.)*

What was wrong with your mother?

MAXINE. She was ... very, very sad.

DESSA. Sad?

MAXINE. Well, I mean, she was also, I don't know, *sick*. Beyond sad. She was insane.

DESSA. So there's some sort of dividing line?

MAXINE. Between sad and crazy? Yeah. It's chemical. She didn't want it.

DESSA. Well, who wants it?

MAXINE. No, I know, but ... she would pass a certain point that most people get to and they turn back, she couldn't. It was like watching someone fall off a cliff, looking back as they fall, a hand goes up and there's nothing to hold on to. *(She looks at DESSA.)* I make a lot up, I think. Stories. To make sense. Give myself a past. Or change it. There's the story ...

DESSA. What story?

MAXINE. If she'd lived. That story. I think about calling her, like on her birthday, and it would be ... so sort of dull and nice ... she would let me tell her what I was up to and then I would listen to what she was up to, you know, how her cats were doing, getting her gutters cleaned, whether she'd put her bulbs in early this year ... you know. And then, this is the thing, I would hang up, yawn, and forget her. Forget about her. Because she would just be my mother, the woman I call once a week. I could take her for granted. I would love her, certainly, but like the way you love your hands, or your knees, if you can call that love, since you don't really think about it. She would just have been my mother. Known so well that I wouldn't know that I didn't know her at all. But I could forget her. Because she didn't forget me.

(They look out their windows in silence.)

Scene 15. Open Eyes.

(Lights remain on MAXINE and DESSA in the cockpit. Lights up on ZOFIA in her chair, looking out. Sound of a plane.)

ZOFIA. I hear you, Maxine, flying tonight.
That sound, I know that sound.
I have listened all day to it.
It is the sound of your open eyes.
Searching the darkness for your lost girl.

And perhaps she is waiting there. The lost one.
Not the one you think you're looking for.
That child is lost forever.
No.
Someone, something else.
The one in the darkness.
She sees you now.
Her face is white with the moon.
She maybe reaches up,
as if she could draw a finger down your shining belly as you
pass above her, raking your beautiful lights across her open
eyes.
Turn back, Maxine.
Close your eyes.
What you are looking for is not what you are looking for.
Learn to lose what should not be found.

(Lights intensify on MAXINE, looking out. There is the sense of movement and presence in the darkness around her. Perhaps we hear snatches of CHARLOTTE's dialogue ("You're stuck in the middle of the rope, right smack in the middle, no going forward, no going back...") and EVIE's ("For

instance, you're looking up at me right now, and let me tell you something, you're right, I'm exactly what you look like ..."). *The sound of the plane's engine peaks, as if going directly over the audience's heads, then cuts out abruptly.*)

END OF ACT I

ACT II

Scene 16. Another Story.

(Lights up on MAXINE and DESSA in the cockpit. Later that same evening. Silence.)

DESSA. Have you ever looked for a child?

MAXINE. No.

DESSA. Not once?

MAXINE. No. It's been mostly hikers—backpackers who get lost. All adults, just barely, some of them, but yeah, no one under eighteen. There have been people, too, who came up to the mountains, came out alone to kill themselves, or said that's what they were going to do.

DESSA. And you found them?

MAXINE. Every single one. Perfect record.

DESSA. Before or after?

MAXINE. What?

DESSA. They killed themselves.

MAXINE. Before. Two different ones. Before.

DESSA. Huh. *(Pause.)* You know what? The first thing they did with me at the police station, once they'd asked all the questions and shit, the first thing they do is I'm strapped up to this polygraph test, really, I couldn't believe it, across the table from this guy. He's asking me, did *I* kidnap her. My own daughter. Did I kill her. The needle's bouncing around on the paper. He keeps saying, "Lady, Lady, it's standard procedure." Incredible. I wanted to kill ... somebody, him, somebody, anybody.

MAXINE. Yeah. But he's right, that's the norm. Abductions of children by strangers are incredibly rare. Children almost always know the person who abducts them.

DESSA. Yeah. I've heard that. And it's a great comfort.

MAXINE. I'm sorry.

(Pause.)

DESSA. They told me all that. First thing. *Very* interested that I don't know exactly who her father is. My whole, like, completely fucked-up personal life just lying on the police linoleum there like puke. They couldn't really get it, that I'd just run like hell, put this huge distance between me and anybody who could have been her father. Out of maybe six guys. Just came up here. Put my finger on the map. I thought, O.K. where in the world is it, like, completely nowhere and nobody knows me. O.K. Loon Lake, that sounds nice. I thought, she'll like that, the baby. Loons. And around it, green map color. Nothing much. Trees. There was that little picture of the tree on the map. Pine trees. And none of those guys will ever know, not that they would care much, I'm not going to flatter myself here, but they wouldn't be able to find me even if they wanted to. And no one ever knew I was pregnant. That I know. Nobody from my life before.

MAXINE. Do you know which of them, I mean, can you guess now, knowing her, what she looks like, can you guess which one of them was the one?

DESSA. She doesn't look like anyone I've ever known. She's completely different.

And whoever took her, whoever that was, she'd never seen him before. I know that. Whoever the fuck that was.

The night after the polygraph test I fell asleep in the, the police station there. I put my head down on the desk and bam, like I'd been slugged on the head. Had the print of somebody's paper clip on my cheek for like two days. But here's the thing. What I dreamt was that I *did* abduct her like they said. I'm telling you, oh God, what an incredible relief. I'd just *forgotten* that I did. And I'm standing at the sink, doing dishes and I'm looking out the window at this little green garden shed out back, it's like falling over, about the size of an outhouse, tiny, you know, and I'm looking at it and I suddenly remember that Charlotte, I put her out there *myself*, in the shed, it was all so, like, well, *of course,* how stupid of me, causing all this trouble, I just forgot.

MAXINE. "Silly me."

DESSA. Yeah. Like that.

(MAXINE slaps her forehead in a gesture of sudden remembrance. DESSA laughs. They begin on a riff that builds, laughing hard and cutting each other off. The laughter should seem disproportionate to the jokes themselves.)

MAXINE. "You won't believe this, Officers,"—

DESSA. —Yeah. "I'm just such a knucklehead"—

MAXINE. —"I'm hoping you'll see the *humor* in this"—

DESSA. —"Turns out, all along"—

MAXINE. —"My mistake"—

DESSA. —"My daughter has been sitting out / in the *garden shed*"—

MAXINE. —"in the *garden shed*"—

(They fall apart, laughing.)

DESSA. —"I can't for the *life* of me think why I put her out there to begin with"—

MAXINE. —"But she's been out there, eating saltines, for, oh, two weeks now." "Oh, / she's fine"—

DESSA. —"Oh, she's *fine*"—"Nothing a couple of decades of therapy can't take care of"—

MAXINE. —"Sorry to bother you"—

DESSA. —"Thousands of dollars in search parties and helicopters, is that right?"—

MAXINE. —"What nice dogs. All the way from Quebec, you say?"—

DESSA. —"Thanks so much for everything. We'll just be going home now"—

MAXINE. *(The topper.)* —"Won't happen again"—

DESSA. Right. "Won't happen again." *(They are exhausted from laughing so hard, and a little stunned. Silence as they look out their respective windows.)* They got dogs from Quebec?

MAXINE. I just made that up.

(They look out their windows. Silence.)

DESSA. You know that story? About calling your mother?

MAXINE. Yeah?

DESSA. I got one too.

See, it's this winter afternoon, a Sunday, right, beautiful day, and Charlotte is getting back from this field trip that she begged me to let her go on, she's got these friends, these girls, and they go on nature walks but I think it's mostly about screaming, you know, the way they laugh, almost peeing their pants from everything being so funny. They never see any wildlife on these things, these expeditions, I think 'cause they make so much noise. But, you know, what the hell, right? I remember that. And it's good for me, I got the whole day. I take all our laundry down to the coin-op and I get, like, nine loads done and between times I'm running around, I shop for the whole week and pick up her shoes from the shoe repair, and all during that day, I'm thinking what a good time she's having. I look up at the mountains from the street there and it all looks so gorgeous. She's up there, I think, laughing like that with all her friends. I make her fried chicken, 'cause I kind of missed her all day, and peas. And when she gets dropped off, she's got some sunburn, not a lot, but from the shine off the snow, you know, and she's kind of like privately exhilarated. She pushes her peas around on the plate and tells me her adventures, goofs on everybody, who threw up on the bus, you know, she sings me a song she just learned, and then she goes to bed sort of early, 'cause tomorrow's school ... And all over the town, the girls are pushing their peas around plates and telling somebody their adventures and then dreaming. They dream about mountains, of their feet stomping snow, about pine trees, about each other. And then they wake up and forget those dreams and their lives just rush past with all the details and daylight until, in this story, they are old, old women who can't remember that song they sang, that trip they took, the names, even, of their first dear friends, or anything at all really except something very vague but good about one afternoon in the bright sun in the snow, when they were all such young, young girls.

(They look out their respective windows.)

Scene 17. The Bear.

(Late night. MAXINE comes into ZOFIA's place, bearing groceries. She sets the bag down and begins unloading it. She opens the refrigerator. It contains nothing except suspicious items balled up in tin foil.)

MAXINE. *(To herself.)* Jesus, Zofia. *(She gingerly takes an item out, unwraps it tentatively, and sniffs it.)* Oh, for goodness sake.

(MAXINE starts throwing items away. ZOFIA enters, unsteadily, holding a baseball bat.)

ZOFIA. Oh. I thought it was a bear in the kitchen. I forgot you were here.

MAXINE. So you often have to club bears in the kitchen?

ZOFIA. Only a few times in the summer, but they sleep in the winter, so I was surprised.

MAXINE. I know you're kidding.

ZOFIA. Oh, good for you.

MAXINE. This does not look like a sane person's refrigerator.

ZOFIA. It's not my fault. Everything goes bad faster now.

MAXINE. What do you eat?

ZOFIA. There's some gingersnaps if you want.

MAXINE. What did you eat today?

ZOFIA. *(Doing American.)* I shot me a moose.

MAXINE. Seriously.

ZOFIA. *(Referring to her body.)* Look at this big hot thing. I eat. Don't worry. Let the bears have it. Just tea. I don't need more. When I was a little girl all I did was eat. And it was never enough. You know what they called me? *Krowka. Mawa krowka.* Little Cow. Because I was always chewing. Like that. *(She chews.)* So, what happened, I ate enough for my whole life then. I don't need any more. I'm done eating. At last.

MAXINE. It doesn't work that way. What did you eat today?

ZOFIA. I forget. But you know what I mean? The way things go bad faster? I look the other way, it can't be very long, I look back ... Such things as this. *(She picks up an apple MAXINE has brought.)* Oh, this will be a terrible wrong thing by noon tomorrow. This can't have been true before. You can't trust anything. Maybe they come into the world older. Like you. Oh, you remind me. I saw your girl.

MAXINE. Who?

ZOFIA. The lost girl. Oh, you've got trouble with her, ach. Such a wild thing. She's been around here. I leave her milk outside, she won't come in. Mostly at night she comes. She likes to play outside the bedroom window. She puts her fingers up and makes shadows on the window. Like this. *(She makes frantic hand signals.)* You can come see if you want. Greasy hands all over the window she leaves. She thinks she's funny, to wake up an old woman. Or she runs past the window there, oh she's a bold thing, she's grinning. She's in the corner of the eye always. Very smart. You look up and whup, she's gone.

MAXINE. What does she look like?

ZOFIA. So dirty, ach. Her big mouth, the jelly stains. I left jelly on a plate. She ate it up. You know I think you're going to have a hard time. She *wants* to be lost like that. She's happy. It was the same with Evie. She knows you're looking for her but every day, every night that goes by she forgets more the ways she used to be. She can't even talk English anymore. Ach. *(She picks up the apple again.)* Maybe she'll like this. Oh, this will be good. I don't know why I care. She's a terrible little girl.
You wait. Maybe tonight. I'll call you when she comes.

MAXINE. You do that.

ZOFIA. Look at you. You're too tired. Go to bed.

MAXINE. I go you go, Pogo.

(MAXINE helps ZOFIA to her feet.)

ZOFIA. *(Laughs.)* I go you go, Pogo. Who said that?

MAXINE. *(They start to exit.)* I did.

ZOFIA. Before you.

MAXINE. You did.

ZOFIA. I did?

MAXINE. Someone I know did.

ZOFIA. *(She looks out the window.)* It was Evie. Sometimes I see her in that tree.

MAXINE. Who?

ZOFIA. *(Dismissively.)* Ach. Little girls.
You fell out of that tree. Do you remember?

MAXINE. No.

ZOFIA. You broke your arm. But you didn't cry. Not even a little. The doctor, he couldn't believe it.

MAXINE. I can see why he'd be puzzled.

ZOFIA. He called you "a little soldier." *(Laughs.)* Do you know what your first sentence was?

MAXINE. No. What?

ZOFIA. "Leave me be."

MAXINE. *(Appalled.)* God.

ZOFIA. You said it all the time. I don't know where you heard that. "Leave me be."

MAXINE. Well. Gosh. Good for me, I guess.

ZOFIA. *(As she exits.)* I thought it was good.

MAXINE. *(Alone.)* Well, it certainly worked.

(A thump, as of a bird hitting a window. She looks up.)

Scene 18. Bed.

(MAXINE sleeps. CHARLOTTE sits bolt upright next to her.)

CHARLOTTE. Did you ever notice how completely like *obsessed* you are with other people eating? "Did you eat?" "Do you eat?" "Do you have any food in the house?" "What did you eat today?" My mother, your grandmother. It's a mania with you.

MAXINE. *(Beleaguered.)* Oh, God.

CHARLOTTE. *I've* noticed.

MAXINE. No wonder I wake up exhausted.

(MAXINE stirs and sits upright, but avoids looking at CHAR-LOTTE.)

CHARLOTTE. What *is* it with you?

MAXINE. Nobody's—everybody's falling apart on me.

CHARLOTTE. Yeah. So you think *eating* is the solution here?

MAXINE. Wouldn't hurt.

CHARLOTTE. How about you? Don't notice you eating much.

MAXINE. I do.

(A bump against the window.)

CHARLOTTE. What was that?

MAXINE. Birds. Starlings, I think. They live in the eaves. Some people have mice. My grandmother has starlings, and apparently bears. The occasional bear.

CHARLOTTE. She was kidding.

MAXINE. One hopes.

CHARLOTTE. And me. She sees me.

MAXINE. Oh, yes, you too. There's a lot going on here.

CHARLOTTE. You think she's crazy.

MAXINE. Oh, she's definitely crazy. I know crazy when I see it.

CHARLOTTE. Uh huh. And what about you?

(Pause. Another thump.)

MAXINE. Please go back to your mother. She's in agony. She misses you so.

CHARLOTTE. Me? *(She snickers.)*
As if I had anything to do with that poor woman. Don't you know whose child I am?

(Another thump.)

MAXINE. I did know that. I do know that.

CHARLOTTE. I'm all yours, Baby.

MAXINE. In other words, you're useless.

CHARLOTTE. —I wouldn't say *that*—

MAXINE. —The girl I'm looking for—

CHARLOTTE. —Oh, *her*—

MAXINE. —She's nothing like you.

CHARLOTTE. Who knows? *(Pause.)* Poor thing.

MAXINE. Why can't I find her?

CHARLOTTE. Poor thing.

MAXINE. *(Cries.)* Why can't I find her?

CHARLOTTE. Where are you looking? *(MAXINE continues to cry. CHARLOTTE examines her. She carefully places a finger in the center of MAXINE's chest. MAXINE keeps her eyes closed.)* Can you feel that?

MAXINE. Yes.

CHARLOTTE. What does it feel like?

MAXINE. Ice. Dead ice. Deep, hard. Stop.

(CHARLOTTE takes her finger away. She then leans down, opens her mouth wide and breathes onto MAXINE's cheek.)

CHARLOTTE. Can you feel that?

MAXINE. Yes.

CHARLOTTE. What does it feel like?

MAXINE. The draft from an open door.

CHARLOTTE. What does it smell like?

MAXINE. Terror.

CHARLOTTE. What does it sound like?

MAXINE. A cry that will not be heard.

CHARLOTTE. *(Leans back.)* Hm. Do you have your eyes closed?

MAXINE. Yes.

CHARLOTTE. Why?

MAXINE. So that I can't see you.

CHARLOTTE. What do you see?

MAXINE. You.

(CHARLOTTE smiles.)

CHARLOTTE. Let me try. *(She closes her eyes.)* Oh, yeah. My own personal night. It's not so bad, blindness. All alone in here.

(CHARLOTTE puts her thumb in her mouth.)

MAXINE. You're too old to be sucking your thumb.

CHARLOTTE. You know I only do it when no one can see me.

MAXINE. You're so cold.

CHARLOTTE. Yeah, well, I'm dying the good death, asleep in a snow drift somewhere. Long, sweet dreams that carry you to oblivion in stately procession like a princess: horses, carriages, quaint townspeople cheering. I'm still a little girl, you're right, this is how I would die.

MAXINE. Wait. I don't want you to go.

CHARLOTTE. But you think she's gone, don't you? Why not this way? This is the best you can hope for.

MAXINE. I know.

CHARLOTTE. It's almost painless.

MAXINE. Still.

CHARLOTTE. You know it's the best possible fate.

MAXINE. I can't yet.

CHARLOTTE. Look at this. It's really kind of lovely.

MAXINE. Even so. I want her alive.

CHARLOTTE. But, Maxine, you know what she could be going through. Anything would be better. And this is such a *nice* death.

MAXINE. I know. Even so. Wake up.

CHARLOTTE. You'll have to do it. I'm too tired.

MAXINE. Wake up.

(MAXINE comes up to a sitting position. Still keeping her eyes closed.)

CHARLOTTE. I'm asleep. Good dreams.

(MAXINE opens her eyes and turns and shakes CHARLOTTE.)

MAXINE. Wake up! Wake up! *(Lights flicker. CHAR-LOTTE disappears. MAXINE is left, sitting upright in bed. She covers her face with her hands.)*
Not yet. *(She sits up, looking out.)*
I'm sorry. Not yet.

(MAXINE looks up.)

Scene 19. Knock Knock.

(EVIE descends.)

EVIE. There was a time—did I tell you?—a time I stole out of my body and slunk up the wall and then in virtuosic escape, up, up, through the corner of that ceiling, through dust and lathing, through a chink in the sliding slate shingles until there ... my final sky, that color blue, at last. And like you I could look down on the world, my body, which I could see now was just awkward temporary housing with faulty plumbing, rats in the attic and crumbling foundations, merely a loan of a house for the distinct spark to live in, where you peer through grimy windows and cannot make out the view of the distant hills.
A rattling, death-bound house that every storm shakes.
And even as I bobbed in the air, even in that vastness and release, all the while the damaged world tugged at my sleeve saying go back, return, land the plane. It is not time. There is more to be done. And the drag and pull was unmistakable, back to the blind husk of the animal housing.
There was nothing to do but to force the shining divinity of myself through a hole in the rotting bird-nested roof and down the rickety attic steps and I could hear the rusted deadbolts sink themselves behind me. And as I stood in the damp, airless room of my particular life, grace slipped my grasp like the strings of balloons and flew up through the soot-caked chimneys.

And I stood again at my own windows peering in pain toward the unseeable hills.

That, my darling, I did. *(MAXINE looks up at her.)*

For you.

MAXINE. I can't do this anymore. I'm losing it. Everything.

Please, just—*(Loud thump.)* What *is* that?

EVIE. Something trying to get in.

MAXINE. It's—

EVIE. —Or something trying to get out.

MAXINE. It sounds familiar.

EVIE. Well, it would. *(EVIE leans down, almost upsidedown over MAXINE, and knocks on the top of her head. We hear it.)* Like that?

MAXINE. Leave me be.

EVIE. As if I could.

MAXINE. Please.

EVIE. Knock knock.

(Pause.)

MAXINE. Who's there?

(EVIE straightens, taking her hand away, and ascends quickly. Just a second too late, MAXINE grabs for her. EVIE ascends out of sight. Three rapid thumps at the window.)

Scene 20. Blood from a Stone.

(Before dawn. MAXINE enters the living room. ZOFIA is there.)

MAXINE. I need you to tell me what happened in this house.

ZOFIA. It was over a long time ago.

MAXINE. It's not over for me. I need to know what happened to Evie.

ZOFIA. You don't remember.

MAXINE. No.

ZOFIA. Good for you.

MAXINE. No, Babcia, no. Not good for me. I'm sick of it. I can't ... I can't do it anymore. It's killing me. You're the only one. You've got to tell me.

(Pause.)

ZOFIA. *(Looks at her for the first time.)* I don't remember.

MAXINE. Of course you do.

ZOFIA. No. I threw it away. All of it. One by one. Her feet, her hands, the way she walked, tilt of her head, her face, her face ... *(She makes the gesture of throwing.)* Everything that happened to her, the whole terrible life of her, everything she did to that body of hers. That body I gave to the world. *(She makes the gesture.)* I threw it all away. It took years. I did that to her. I killed her in my head. I had to. Because of what she did to me. What is left of her? *(She snaps her fingers.)* Just that. It took a long time.

MAXINE. So you can't give me anything.

ZOFIA. *(Shrugs.)* Blood from a stone, you can't get it.

MAXINE. Blood from a stone.

ZOFIA. I don't remember her.

MAXINE. *(Vehement.)* I don't believe you.

(MAXINE leaves.)

Scene 21. Still Buzzing.

(Across a vast, white, vacant field, CHARLOTTE stumbles. She is bloody and dirty. A plane is heard buzzing. She looks up. She puts her hands over her face. The buzzing stops. She takes her hands away, the buzzing continues. The plane is still there, louder now. She is looking up.)

CHARLOTTE. Ma? Mama?

(Lights up on MAXINE, asleep at the table in the airplane hangar. DESSA stands beside her. MAXINE wakes with a jolt. The buzzing stops.)

MAXINE. I had to come down for gas.
DESSA. Uh huh.
MAXINE. And the snow. I couldn't see anymore.
DESSA. It's coming down.
MAXINE. I couldn't see.
DESSA. I know. I just ... I couldn't stay in the house anymore. She's not there. She's so absolutely *not ... there. (She sits.)* I started screaming. I thought I'd give that a try. I'm sick of crying. It's just exhausting now. It used to, well, it didn't make me feel *better* exactly, but you know, when you do it four, five hours straight, and it's kind of amazing that you *can*, you know, physically do that, at the end of it, I kind of felt, I used to feel *different* at least, washed out, changed. It was a lot like *do*ing something. But now it just feels like throwing up, it's not ... So I tried screaming today.
MAXINE. How'd it go?
DESSA. *(Holds her neck.)* I ripped my throat up. *(She laughs, MAXINE laughs with her. Silence.)*
There isn't a sound I can make that is up to it. This.
What's killing me ...

(DESSA loses her train of thought.)

MAXINE. What's killing you?

DESSA. What's killing me is I drive this school bus, right, and I was so happy to get this job when I got it. It's a cinch, you pick them up and drive them all there and then you got the whole day until you take them all home again. I think what it is is there are just so many more kids than there used to be, too many, and you see these mothers, all these young mothers and everybody's pregnant now, they're all over the place, the supermarket, on the street ... there can't have been that many before, and then there are going to be even *more* kids, dropping their mittens and climbing up that high, tough first step onto the bus, and they're all yelling at each other and kicking and punching and running down the aisle and you know that then *those* ones will get together and be breeding more and putting *theirs* on the bus, which I'll still be driving,'cause what the hell else will ever happen to me, and so I look at these pregnant women, the like, *battalions* of them and I want them, I want to scream at them to just stop, if they'd just *stop,* you know? Basta. No more. This whole fucking planet, this is what it feels like, it's just a fucking *mess.* These whores and assholes and nobody's paying any attention.

MAXINE. To what?

DESSA. *(Startled to be in the midst of conversation.)* The truth.

MAXINE. Which is?

DESSA. There is this, this ... evil ... it's waiting, it, you can't, there's nothing you can do about it. I want it, this whole fucking thing, this earth, to just stop. Just stop. Let it snow for awhile. So it's quiet. So I can think. *(Pause.)*
There can be nothing worse than this. Nothing will ever compare to this. My own death? It's gonna be a fucking picnic.

MAXINE. Piece of cake.

DESSA. Right. Compared to this.

MAXINE. Well ... at least you know that. You know it can't get any worse than this.

DESSA. *(Looks at MAXINE.)* Oh. I think it probably can.

Scene 22. The Glint.

(MAXINE in the cockpit.)

MAXINE. You can stop that world, the whole of it, flying, howling as you fly, tears and ice freezing to your open eyes, you can search the globe for that one child and if you are what you are, which is the great grieving goddess of that creation, you will stop that world, place a finger on that spinning globe and all ceases—no more of the reckless movement and cursed rush of life. The rivers freeze, the trees drop their distracting, obfuscating leaves and all land and all sea chill to bone, ash, the color of visibility. And the land betrays its true contours in death and sleeping. Wait, wait, you say, nothing will happen until this one thing happens, until this one precious individual thing, my only thing, the only color allowed is found. All nature subdued, all sound gone until you hear the pulse, the only pulse, of that girl.
If you could do that you would.
Time unticked. Years that she isn't getting older, learning to play an instrument, use a compass, fall in love—those years would not go by.
That child, that girl is the silent globe itself, locked on its axis, tilting her head, her eyes glittering, staring at the finally fixed stars which tell her stories of light that are too ancient to mean anything. And there in that stopped, hushed place between stars and their planets, in that perpetual present of her absence, there, there, you would find her.
Charlotte. Charlotte. My child. Today is the day.

(A blinding flash. A violent noise. Blackness and then whiteness. Silence. MAXINE stands on that white vastness that CHARLOTTE walked across and howls, a screaming howl of grief.)

Scene 23. The Finding.

*(DESSA waits in the airplane hangar. MAXINE enters, look-
ing destroyed and violently disheveled.)*

DESSA. You found her.
MAXINE. Yes. So they told you.
DESSA. Yes.
MAXINE. I'm—
DESSA. —Of course you are. *(Pause. MAXINE shifts her
weight.)* And I don't want to be touched. *(Pause.)* You can do
something for me.
MAXINE. Please.
DESSA. Tell me. How it, what she, what you saw.
MAXINE. I saw it. The glint. It was the upturned window.
The truck was rolled on its side so the window, a part of it that
wasn't covered with snow, it glinted. I circled it twice, no,
three times, it was three times, and I, I basically, I crashed the
plane is what it amounts to. I was lucky, but I'd gotten too
close and the downdraft of the mountain ... I mean I managed
to get it down but it won't be flying again. So I got out of it
and I ... started running ... for that place, I just wasn't thinking, I did everything wrong, I didn't radio ... it was stupid ... I
ran, I don't know how long it took, I ran to that place and I got
up there. The truck was deep in a gully at an odd angle, it had
hit a tree and I stood on the door, there was someone in there
and I couldn't get the damn thing open, so I think I, yeah, I
kicked through the window, broke the glass and he was in
there, dead, he must have died on impact. He'd been dead a
long time and she wasn't there. Not a trace of her. And I'm
standing on the door and I suddenly realize that there are tracks,
you can barely make them out, but tracks, and they run, they're
small, they run quite precisely in a neat line to the edge of a

cliff. Couldn't be more than twenty paces and then ... So I got on my belly and looked over ...

DESSA. What did you see?

MAXINE. Your daughter was ... her body ... she was lodged in a tree. She had broken down through, in her fall she'd broken down through the first tiers of a very tall pine tree and she was hanging there. Her arms are outstretched and her head is back, tilted up.

DESSA. Are her eyes open?

MAXINE. Yes.

DESSA. Is she bloody?

MAXINE. No. She is not at all bloody.

(Pause.)

DESSA. Is that possible?

MAXINE. *(She thinks for a moment.)* I think it must be.

(Long pause.)

DESSA. I waited for you. They didn't want me to come with them to see her. They didn't tell me anything except that she was dead and that you'd found her. They didn't tell me. I knew you would. *(Pause.)*

And I'm grateful, or something, I guess. But I think, I think I also, very much, um, hate you. *(Surprised that she's identified an emotion.)* Yes. I do. *(Pause.)*

They're bringing her back.

MAXINE. It's going to take awhile.

(Pause.)

DESSA. I think I can wait.

(Pause.)

MAXINE. Dessa. Would you mind if I stayed here with

you? Until they bring her back?
    DESSA. Just don't ask me if I'll be all right.
    MAXINE. I won't.
    DESSA. I will never be all right. Never again.
And we will not speak. Never again.

(They wait.)

Scene 24. The Return.

(MAXINE enters ZOFIA's. Very late. ZOFIA sits, as usual, staring out.)

    ZOFIA. This is the last night, I think.
    MAXINE. Yes. I found her. She's dead.

(MAXINE crumples down next to ZOFIA. ZOFIA strokes her hair.)

    ZOFIA. *(Soothing.)* Poor little one. Poor little one.
    MAXINE. I've lost my plane, Babcia. I crashed it. My sweet old Cessna. I've lost everything.
    ZOFIA. It is possible. To lose everything. It can be done.
I looked out the window all day and I thought of you. This cold, this long winter and it doesn't seem possible that the world can ever be returned to us. Life has turned its face away. But much is promised.
Spring, they say. She will come back. And the world will be a wild green place again.
It has been promised. So perhaps it's true.
And more, even, is promised to us ...
I lied to you. I remember everything. I see her now. I see her always. My Evie. And always now she is walking up the road, coming back to me like she did those mornings. Her hair is wet and filled with new torn leaves and she combs her red fingers through it and hums, holding her shoes in her hand.

She looks so tired and calm, so thin ... And she has seen too much.
But she is coming home.
And so I think somehow I will touch her again, warm her
hands, and she will tell me of her adventures.
Perhaps, after all, it is possible.
They say there will be a spring and a returning.
Perhaps all the lost ones will be called to home.
And I would like to believe it. If only for you.
My little soldier. My little Maxine.
Go to sleep.
In the morning you will go back to your life.

*(MAXINE embraces ZOFIA. MAXINE exits. ZOFIA stares,
directly ahead.)*

Scene 25. Last.

(EVIE hangs, as at first, over MAXINE's bed.)

MAXINE. There was someone who was my mother. A hand
on my head, doing buttons down my back, nudging shoes onto
my feet, she was ... whoever she was, she was my mother ...
You can tell me ... You can tell me now. Why. Why she left me.

EVIE. You don't remember.

MAXINE. No.

EVIE. I remember you. Your little eyes, always on me. What
terrible luck for you, to have chosen me. As if I could have
been your mother, pulled it off.

MAXINE. But you were. You did.

EVIE. Oh, I could fool myself sometimes. Sunny days, one
or two, when I would watch other women, mothers hauling
their children by their thin arms around the produce sections,
and I'd think, oh, *that's* how it's done, I can do that, certainly.
No one need know, not even you, about the black nights of

sleeplessness, the screaming voices in my ears, the way my face would distort itself into the monster I knew I was when I looked up from bathing you into the fogged light of the bathroom mirror. You see, it was hopeless.

MAXINE. You could have. I loved you enough.

EVIE. It had nothing to do with love. There was not enough of a mother in me to hold you. Plant my feet like roots in dirt though I did, weight my breasts with your milk, the night would come and pluck me by the hair like a farmer rips a weed from the ground and then I was yanked high and howling once again. Even you couldn't save me from it. Circling in my terrible burning plane, oil flames licking the glass as I looked down on that cherished place where there was no landing night after night.

MAXINE. What did you see from your plane?

EVIE. There were two perfect hills, burnished and smooth, seamed with the fringe of two perfect lines: Your closed eyes, nights when I leaned over you, breathing my dragon breath on your curved cheek. The hills shudder and pulse, holding your dreams of milk and blankets. Your lashes quiver like feathers on a sleeping bird. But up above you in the black sky a plane is circling, burning badly, engine exploding, tin and glass shrieking, circling above you, far too close for comfort. Until the pilot finally pulls herself away at last, spins out into the night alone. I thought, keep me from her, God. Let me let her live.

MAXINE. I was dreaming of you.

EVIE. No doubt. And in those dreams you found a mother I could leave you with. Because I could not stay.

MAXINE. So you left me to miss you for the rest of my life.

EVIE. I knew it would be better.

MAXINE. How could you know? How could you possibly know? I have spent myself in yearning. Yearned for you, searched all my life for you without ever finding any trace of you. I have no place in the world. I am an exile, wandering around endlessly, looking for a woman I can't even remember.

There is no compensation for the loss you gave me from the very beginning. None. No true comfort. Just searching. And long nights. And when I dream, I dream of you. You have destroyed me. I never had a chance.

EVIE. You have had a chance. I gave it to you. That's the only thing I've ever done. Give you that. And you do remember me. You know what I did for you.

MAXINE. I remember nothing.

EVIE. It was a particular morning. Still before light. A morning. Very much like this one. You remember.

MAXINE. I don't.

EVIE. Bad times had come again. Sleep would never come again. I had walked the floor all night long. You must have heard me.

MAXINE. I didn't.

EVIE. My teeth chattering from terror. Talking to all the others. They were all there. You must have heard us.

MAXINE. I didn't, no.

EVIE. We leaned over you once more. Breathed one last time on your perfect cheek. You must have felt it. We decided, we discussed it amongst us. There had to be a choice. And I did what I thought was the noble thing. I chose you.

(Long pause.)

MAXINE. I hate you.

EVIE. So I climbed up all the stairs to the top of this terrible house. Like a mountain climber. Coil of musty rope across my back. You must have heard me. Thump, thump, thump.

MAXINE. Stop this.

(MAXINE puts her hands over her ears.)

EVIE. Stood on your grandfather's crumbling wooden chair. Threw the rope up, once, twice, at least twice. You must have heard.

MAXINE. Stop.

EVIE. It was ridiculously hard to do. Truly improbable. The chair swaying. That rotten rafter ...

MAXINE. This isn't what I wanted to know.

EVIE. And those clumsy knots. Who knew?

MAXINE. Not this.

EVIE. Who knew it would work?

MAXINE. This is nowhere in my head.

EVIE. *(Vehement.)* It is the center stone of the whole damn orbiting mess.

MAXINE. I would remember that.

EVIE. *Yes. You would.* Your open, open eyes. Because you climbed those stairs too. Just like me, on your little short legs. Wearing your torn nightgown, which caught on the splinters. You remember.

MAXINE. I don't.

EVIE. Oh yes. *(Pause.)* Because you found me.

(Pause.)

MAXINE. I found you.

(Pause.)

EVIE. You found me. Of course.

MAXINE. Of course.

(Silence.)

EVIE. There was a window, and you turned to it after. You looked out. And then this, all these years.

(EVIE plucks at her clothes.)

MAXINE. Look at you.

EVIE. It was the best you could do.

MAXINE. *(Suddenly fierce.) Go.* Go, if you're going.
I dressed you for travel years ago and you have gone nowhere.
    EVIE. I can't. I am yours.

(Pause.)

    MAXINE. I wish I didn't love you.
    EVIE. If wishes were fishes ...
    MAXINE. Because then I wouldn't keep you anymore.
    EVIE. Love?
    MAXINE. Always. Still. All right. Enough. *(MAXINE climbs up on the headboard of her bed. She gently pulls on her mother's foot, bringing the body slowly down. They finally stand, face to face, on the bed.)*
Enough.
Let me get this off you at last.

(MAXINE takes the aviator goggles, helmet and dust coat off her mother, revealing an ordinary woman in a housedress. EVIE slowly collapses onto the bed, into MAXINE's embrace. MAXINE sits, her back against the headboard, cradling her mother in her arms.)

    EVIE. When I died, I died thinking of you. It was just the two of us. We were traveling. But we couldn't hold hands because we were flying, like birds, feathers and all, wide wings pumping through the blue. I couldn't see you, but I knew you were behind me, and I was glad because, my God, the landscape was so beautiful. Mountains like fabric puckered and plucked from a table, the glint of rivers singing their veins through the mottled green. And I knew you were seeing it too. And I was happy. I thought, well, at least I've given her something.
Because you were right behind me, coming along.

(EVIE's body goes limp. Her eyes close.)

MAXINE. There is a hole in me, Mama, big as the sky. It's the hole that you made in your passage out of the world. Passage you could not make except through me. I look up and there it is, I recognize it. It's that big, Mama. I think maybe it goes on forever.
But I put you in it, winged. Because I will have you somehow, even there, even so. Even if your natural element can only be the terrible aching vastness which is your absence from me.

(MAXINE is holding EVIE in her arms. She lays her mother's body out on the bed carefully, then covers it. Lights up on ZOFIA, staring out. CHARLOTTE, dressed in her own clothes, unbloody, appears. She and ZOFIA look at each other. MAXINE opens her arms in a gesture of release and looks up. At that same moment, CHARLOTTE turns her back to the audience and lifts her arms, as if taking flight. The sound of wings.)

END OF PLAY

POLISH PRONUNCIATION

1. P. 11.
   "Babcia" ("Grandmother")
   Pronounced: Bobcha

2. P. 13.
   "Biedny malutki ptaszek" ("Poor little bird")
   Pronounced: biedneh malootki pitashek

3. P. 14.
   "Ciastko czekoladowe" (Chocolate cake")
   Pronounced: chahstko chekolaoveh

4. P. 23.
   "Czarownica" ("Witch")
   Pronounced: Charrovnitza

5. P. 23.
   "Masz to ve krwi" ("It's in the blood")
   Pronounced: Mahsh toh ve krevee

6. P. 44.
   "Mawa krowka" ("Little Cow")
   Pronounced: Mahwah kroovka

Also By

Ellen McLaughlin
A NARROW BED

Loved by audiences and critics nationwide, this compassionate and reflective play about two women coping with loneliness and loss was also successfully presented Off Broadway. The women are the last members of a rural commune founded in the 60's. One's husband was killed in Vietnam and she still clings to his memory. The other's wisecracking husband is hospitalized and dying. Both women find the courage to accept their "narrow bed" and get on with their lives.

"McLaughlin is a good writer who writes good talk; ... the large chunks of soliloquy are interesting and moving. Women will surely love this play ... [of] such welcome warmth. "
– *New York Post*

"A penetrating study of friendship and idealism under stress."
– *New York Times*

ANON
Kate Robin

Drama / 2m, 12f / Area

Anon. follows two couples as they cope with sexual addiction. Trip and Allison are young and healthy, but he's more interested in his abnormally large porn collection than in her. While they begin to work through both of their own sexual and relationship hang-ups, Trip's parents are stuck in the roles they've been carving out for years in their dysfunctional marriage. In between scenes with these four characters, 10 different women, members of a support group for those involved with individuals with sex addiction issues, tell their stories in monologues that are alternately funny and harrowing..

In addition to Anon., Robin's play What They Have was also commissioned by South Coast Repertory. Her plays have also been developed at Manhattan Theater Club, Playwrights Horizons, New York Theatre Workshop, The Eugene O'Neill Theater Center's National Playwrights Conference, JAW/West at Portland Center Stage and Ensemble Studio Theatre. Television and film credits include "Six Feet Under" (writer/supervising producer) and "Coming Soon." Robin received the 2003 Princess Grace Statuette for playwriting and is an alumna of New Dramatists.

WHITE BUFFALO
Don Zolidis

Drama / 3m, 2f (plus chorus)/ Unit Set

Based on actual events, WHITE BUFFALO tells the story of the miracle birth of a white buffalo calf on a small farm in southern Wisconsin. When Carol Gelling discovers that one of the buffalo on her farm is born white in color, she thinks nothing more of it than a curiosity. Soon, however, she learns that this is the fulfillment of an ancient prophecy believed by the Sioux to bring peace on earth and unity to all mankind. Her little farm is quickly overwhelmed with religious pilgrims, bringing her into contact with a culture and faith that is wholly unfamiliar to her. When a mysterious businessman offers to buy the calf for two million dollars, Carol is thrown into doubt about whether to profit from the religious beliefs of others or to keep true to a spirituality she knows nothing about.

TREASURE ISLAND
Ken Ludwig

All Groups / Adventure / 10m, 1f (doubling) / Areas

Based on the masterful adventure novel by Robert Louis Stevenson, *Treasure Island* is a stunning yarn of piracy on the tropical seas. It begins at an inn on the Devon coast of England in 1775 and quickly becomes an unforgettable tale of treachery and mayhem featuring a host of legendary swashbucklers including the dangerous Billy Bones (played unforgettably in the movies by Lionel Barrymore), the sinister two-timing Israel Hands, the brassy woman pirate Anne Bonney, and the hideous form of evil incarnate, Blind Pew. At the center of it all are Jim Hawkins, a 14-year-old boy who longs for adventure, and the infamous Long John Silver, who is a complex study of good and evil, perhaps the most famous hero-villain of all time. Silver is an unscrupulous buccaneer-rogue whose greedy quest for gold, coupled with his affection for Jim, cannot help but win the heart of every soul who has ever longed for romance, treasure and adventure.

BLUE YONDER
Kate Aspengren

Dramatic Comedy / Monolgues and scenes
12f (can be performed with as few as 4 with doubling) / Unit Set

A familiar adage states, "Men may work from sun to sun, but women's work is never done." In Blue Yonder, the audience meets twelve mesmerizing and eccentric women including a flight instructor, a firefighter, a stuntwoman, a woman who donates body parts, an employment counselor, a professional softball player, a surgical nurse professional baseball player, and a daredevil who plays with dynamite among others. Through the monologues, each woman examines her life's work and explores the career that she has found. Or that has found her.

SKIN DEEP
Jon Lonoff

Comedy / 2m, 2f / Interior Unit Set

In *Skin Deep*, a large, lovable, lonely-heart, named Maureen Mulligan, gives romance one last shot on a blind-date with sweet awkward Joseph Spinelli; she's learned to pepper her speech with jokes to hide insecurities about her weight and appearance, while he's almost dangerously forthright, saying everything that comes to his mind. They both know they're perfect for each other, and in time they come to admit it.

They were set up on the date by Maureen's sister Sheila and her husband Squire, who are having problems of their own: Sheila undergoes a non-stop series of cosmetic surgeries to hang onto the attractive and much-desired Squire, who may or may not have long ago held designs on Maureen, who introduced him to Sheila. With Maureen particularly vulnerable to both hurting and being hurt, the time is ripe for all these unspoken issues to bubble to the surface.

"Warm-hearted comedy … the laughter was literally show-stopping. A winning play, with enough good-humored laughs and sentiment to keep you smiling from beginning to end."
– *TalkinBroadway.com*

"It's a little Paddy Chayefsky, a lot Neil Simon and a quick-witted, intelligent voyage into the not-so-tranquil seas of middle-aged love and dating. The dialogue is crackling and hilarious; the plot simple but well-turned; the characters endearing and quirky; and lurking beneath the merriment is so much heartache that you'll stand up and cheer when the unlikely couple makes it to the inevitable final clinch."
– *NYTheatreWorld.Com*

CPSIA information can be obtained at www.ICGtesting.com
Printed in the USA
LVOW05s1636240114

370879LV00030B/908/P